15.95

D1595242

15.95

Down the Crawfish Hole

Down the Crawfish Hole

Written and Illustrated
by Wes Thomas

PELICAN PUBLISHING COMPANY
Gretna 2004

*The word "Pelican" and the depiction of a pelican are trademarks
of Pelican Publishing Company, Inc., and are registered
in the U.S. Patent and Trademark Office.*

Library of Congress Cataloging-in-Publication Data

Thomas, Wes, 1972-
    Down the crawfish hole / written and illustrated by Wes Thomas.
        p. cm.
    Summary: While fishing on the bayou, Maurice sees a little blue
crawfish drop a watch, follows him down a crawfish hole, and embarks
on an adventure reminiscent of Lewis Carroll's Alice's adventures in
Wonderland.
    ISBN 1-58980-163-6 (hardcover : alk. paper)
    [1. Crayfish—Fiction. 2. Animals—Fiction. 3. Bayous—Fiction.] I.
Title.

PZ7.T369454 2004
[E]—dc22

2003018916

Printed in China

Published by Pelican Publishing Company, Inc.
1000 Burmaster Street, Gretna, Louisiana 70053

This is for my mother with a special thanks to K.R.
I'll keep on searching.

Maurice was beginning to get very sleepy. He and his brother had been fishing on the edge of the bayou all morning. All of a sudden a little blue crawfish jumped out of the weeds.

The crawfish pulled out a watch and cried, "I'm late! I'm late! That old Toad Queen is going to throw me in her pot and boil me!" Then the crawfish scrambled through the grass and leaped into a large crawfish hole.

Maurice noticed that the crawfish had dropped his watch, so he picked it up and followed the crawfish down the large hole. Maurice began to tumble down through a long tunnel! He saw a jar of pralines falling along with him.

Maurice crashed on a bed of oyster shells. He dusted himself off and realized that he was in a large room. In the room were a table and chair that were much larger than he was.

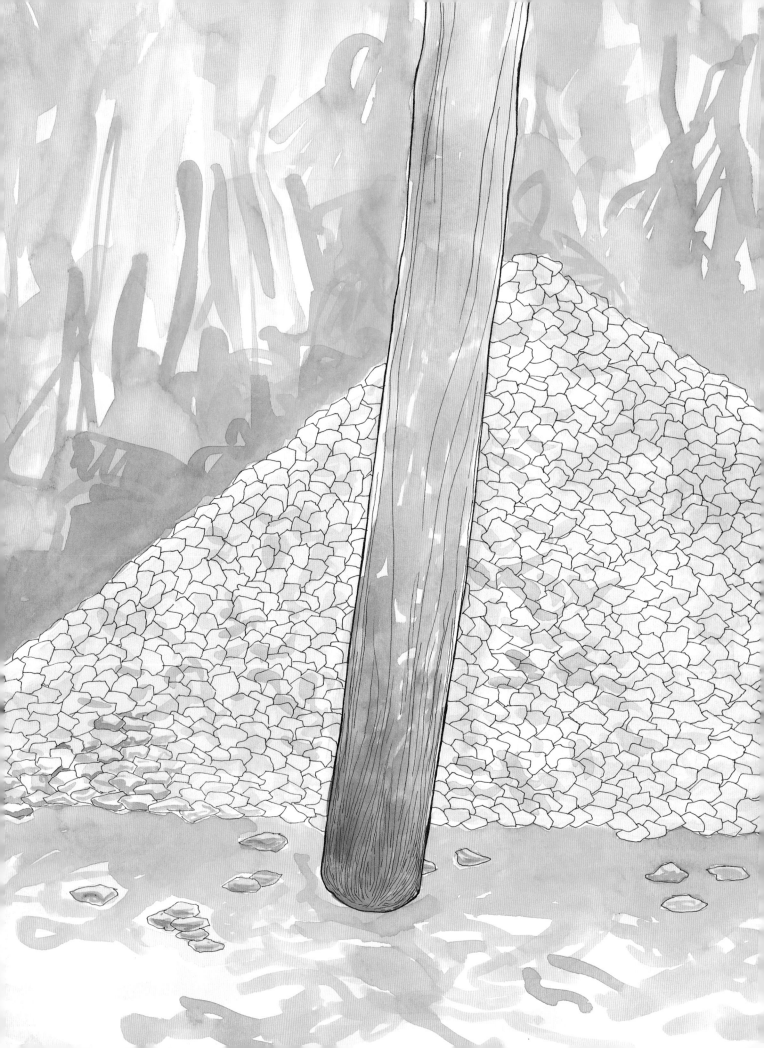

The pralines that had fallen alongside him were scattered on the floor. Maurice saw a little door in the corner of the room, but he was too big to fit through it. He was getting hungry, so he ate one of the pralines that lay on the floor.

After he finished the praline he began to grow very large. He grew so large that he was able to see a bowl of gumbo sitting upon the table. There was a note attached to the bowl that said *EAT ME*. Maurice was still hungry, so he ate the entire bowl of gumbo.

When he had finished eating the gumbo he grew very small. Maurice was so small that he would now be able to fit through the tiny door. Before he left, he picked up the pralines from the floor and put them in his knapsack.

When Maurice opened the door, a garden of strange vegetables appeared before him. In the center he saw an armadillo digging a hole. "Hello, armadillo," Maurice said.

Maurice's voice frightened the armadillo so much that he ran behind some weeds. "You scared me so!" said the armadillo. "What do you want?"

"I'm trying to find a little blue crawfish," Maurice said.

The armadillo replied, "There are no more crawfish around here! The Toad Queen captured every last one and threw them in her pot for stealing her precious pralines. However, one crawfish was set free by the Toad Queen and ordered to bring back her pralines.

"The crawfish said that neither he nor the other crawfish had stolen her pralines, but he would find out who did and bring them before the queen." The armadillo started to dig again and paid no more attention to Maurice.

Maurice saw a little pirogue on the edge of a small lake. He walked towards the boat and noticed a note on the side of it. The note said:

Dear Maurice, take this boat across the lake. I will be with the Toad Queen at her pond. She heard that you had fallen down the great hole and would like to help you get home to your family. Sincerely, Little Blue Crawfish.

Maurice
jumped in the
pirogue and paddled
for almost an hour until he
reached the other side of the lake.
There he spotted a trapper's shack
with a light on inside.

Maurice peeked inside the window and saw an old trapper and an alligator eating supper together. Maybe they know where the crawfish is, thought Maurice.

He was about to knock on the door when all of a sudden the old trapper and the alligator burst out of it and started laughing wildly at Maurice. "Oh, we gave him a good scare!" said the trapper.

"We sure did!" agreed the alligator. Maurice
gulped and asked the two if they had seen a little
blue crawfish, but they only laughed louder. As
the alligator and trapper were laughing
and rolling about on the ground,
Maurice heard a whisper
in the trees.

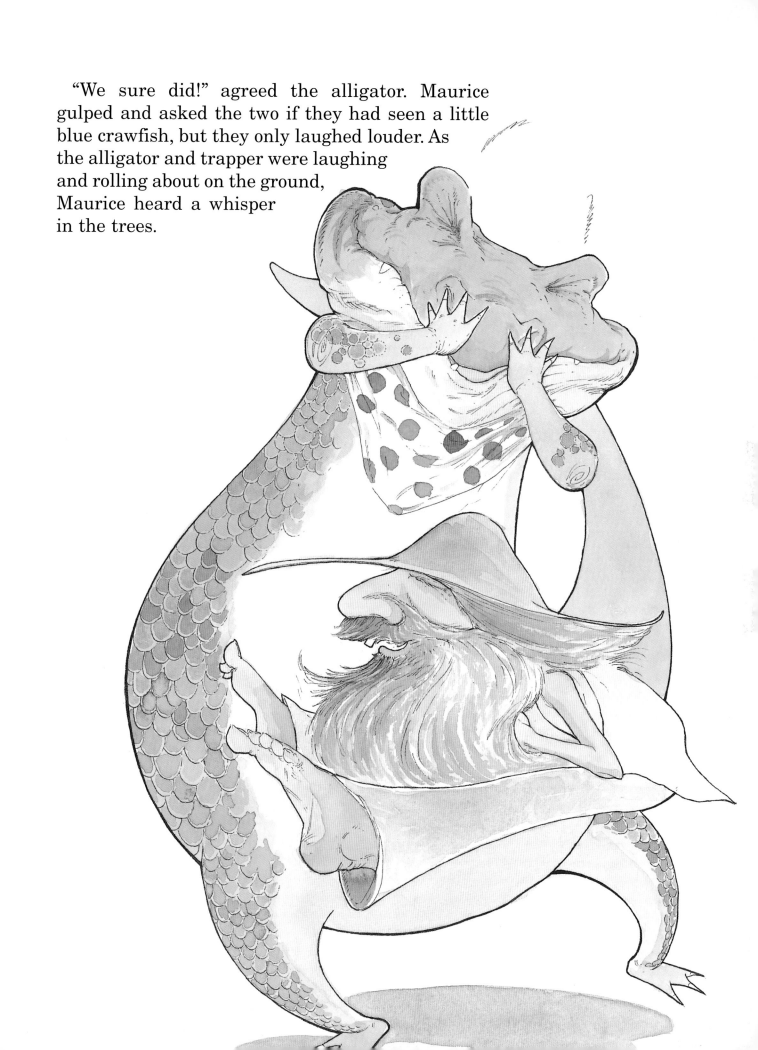

"I'll tell you where the crawfish is," said the voice.
Maurice looked up in the trees and saw a pair of glowing yellow eyes. "Who's there?" he asked.

"Why, the opossum, of course," the voice answered. With a great big grin on his face, the opossum continued, "The crawfish went down the old trail, but beware, for he is a tricky fellow and is always getting into trouble!" When the opossum finished speaking, he disappeared.

Maurice hurried along the old path that twisted and turned through the swamp. Finally he came to a great big pond where many toads were hopping about in all directions. "Capture that boy!" screeched a very loud voice from the center of the pond.

Suddenly Maurice found himself being attacked by hundreds of toads. "Here is your thief, Your Majesty. This boy stole your precious pralines!" one of them yelled. The toads carried Maurice to the center of the pond.

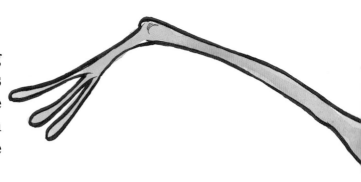

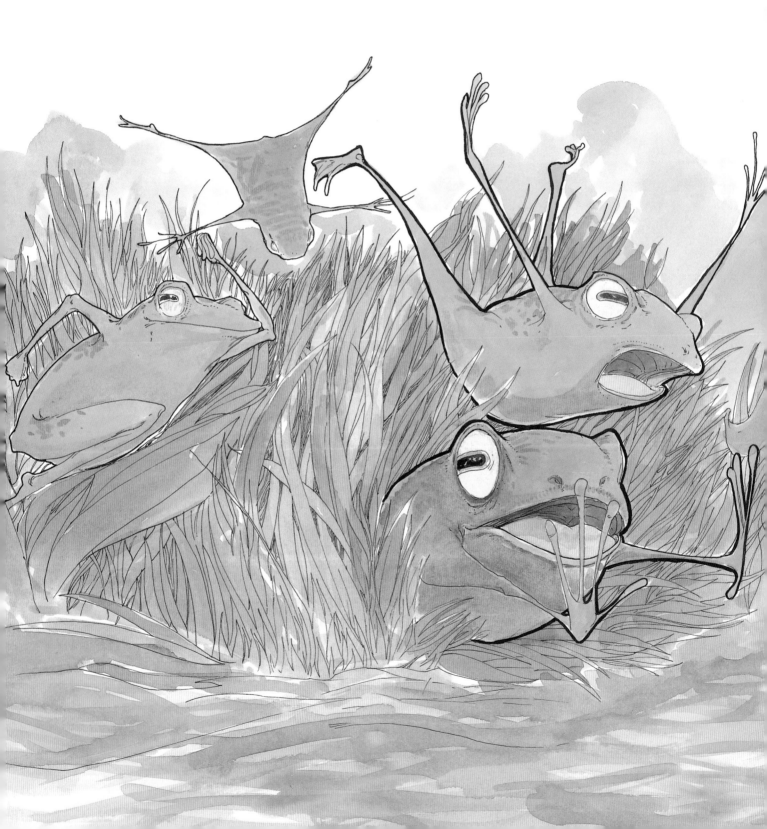

There sat a very old, very fat, and very angry toad. Poking out his head from behind the toad was the little blue crawfish.

"Well, boy, what do you have to say for yourself?" croaked the queen.

"I'm innocent!" cried Maurice.

"He is lying, Your Majesty. I saw him steal the pralines from me and put them in his knapsack," said the crawfish.

"Throw him in the pot!" the Toad Queen screamed.

As Maurice was dragged towards the boiling pot, he grabbed one of the pralines from his knapsack. He ate it quickly and then began to grow.

He grew so large that all the animals, including the Toad Queen, fled in terror.

Suddenly, Maurice heard a voice calling out his name.

"Hey, Maurice, you have a bite. Don't lose it!"

Maurice awoke to find his fishing pole being tugged away by a great big catfish. His brother grabbed the pole and pulled in the fish.

"I just had an amazing dream!" exclaimed Maurice. He told his brother about his dream of falling down the crawfish hole and the adventures he had.

As Maurice was getting ready for bed that evening, he emptied his pockets and a little watch fell to the floor. He picked up the watch and looked at it for a moment. He turned the watch over and saw a name on the back. It read: *Little Blue Crawfish*.